Hello, Family Members,

Learning to read is one of the most important accomplishments of early childhood. **Hello Reader!** books are designed to help children become skilled readers who like to read. Beginning readers learn to read by remembering frequently used words like "the," "is," and "and"; by using phonics skills to decode new words; and by interpreting picture and text clues. These books provide both the stories children enjoy and the structure they need to read fluently and independently. Here are suggestions for helping your child *before*, *during*, and *after* reading:

Before

- Look at the cover and pictures and have your child predict what the story is about.
- Read the story to your child.
- Encourage your child to chime in with familiar words and phrases.
- Echo read with your child by reading a line first and having your child read it after you do.

During

- Have your child think about a word he or she does not recognize right away. Provide hints such as "Let's see if we know the sounds" and "Have we read other words like this one?"
- Encourage your child to use phonics skills to sound out new words.
- Provide the word for your child when more assistance is needed so that he or she does not struggle and the experience of reading with you is a positive one.
- Encourage your child to have fun by reading with a lot of expression . . . like an actor!

After

- Have your child keep lists of interesting and favorite words.
- Encourage your child to read the books over and over again. Have him or her read to brothers, sisters, grandparents, and even teddy bears. Repeated readings develop confidence in young readers.
- Talk about the stories. Ask and answer questions. Share ideas about the funniest and most interesting characters and events in the stories.

I do hope that you and your child enjoy this book.

—Francie Alexander
Reading Specialist,
Scholastic's Instructional Publishing Group

To Emma and Sam,
and to my dad, who helped
me make my first pumpkin man
— J.M.

Cut-paper photography by Paul Dyer

Copyright © 1998 by Judith Moffatt.
All rights reserved. Published by Scholastic Inc.
SCHOLASTIC, HELLO READER!, CARTWHEEL BOOKS and associated logos
are trademarks and/or registered trademarks of Scholastic Inc.

Library of Congress Cataloging-in-Publication Data
Moffatt, Judith.
    The pumpkin man / by Judith Moffatt.
      p.   cm.— (Hello reader! Level 2)
    "Cartwheel books."
    Summary: Children stuff old clothes with autumn leaves, add gloves
and boots and a carved pumpkin head with a light inside, and thus make a
pumpkin man with a happy glowing face. Includes instructions for making a
pumpkin man.
    ISBN 0-590-63865-3
    [1. Pumpkin—Fiction. 2. Jack-o'-lanterns—Fiction.   3. Stories in rhyme.]
I. Title. II. Series.
PZ8.3.M716Pu 1998
[E]—dc21   98-21324
                                             CIP
                                           AC

12 11 10 9 8 7 6 5 4 3 2   8 9/9 0/0 01 02 03

Printed in the U.S.A.   24
First printing, October 1998

THE PUMPKIN MAN

by Judith Moffatt

Hello Reader! — Level 2

SCHOLASTIC INC.  Cartwheel B·O·O·K·S ®

New York Toronto London Auckland Sydney

We go outside.
We rake the leaves.
We pile them way up high.

We jump on top.
We toss them up
and watch the colors fly.

What can we do
with all these leaves?
I know. I have a plan.

We run inside
and find old clothes.

We'll make a pumpkin man.

We button all the buttons.
We tie up legs and sleeves.

We fill and stuff the body
with lots of crunchy leaves.

We give him gloves.
We give him boots.
We're having so much fun.

It's time to pick
a pumpkin head.
We'll find the
nicest one.

Some are short
and some are tall.

Some are bumpy.
Some are small.

We look around
the pumpkin patch.

We find the best of all!

Pumpkins

We cut the top
to get inside.
We scoop out
all the seeds.

We draw a face
and cut it out.
A light is all it needs.

We go outside
at sunset,

put the pumpkin
head in place.

Our pumpkin man smiles back at us with a happy, glowing face.